CLEVELAND
BROWNS

BY JOSH ANDERSON

Stride

An Imprint of The Child's World®

childsworld.com

Published by The Child's World®
800-599-READ • www.childsworld.com

ISBN Information
9781503857766 (Reinforced Library Binding)
9781503860452 (Portable Document Format)
9781503861817 (Online Multi-user eBook)
9781503863170 (Electronic Publication)

LCCN 2021952622

Printed in the United States of America

TABLE OF CONTENTS

GO BROWNS!

The Cleveland Browns compete in the National Football **League's** (NFL's) American Football Conference (AFC). They play in the AFC North **division**, along with the Baltimore Ravens, Pittsburgh Steelers, and Cincinnati Bengals. The Browns have never won a Super Bowl, but the team was one of the best in the 1950s and 1960s. That was before the merger of the NFL and the American Football League (AFL). Let's learn more about the Browns!

AFC NORTH DIVISION

Baltimore Ravens

Cincinnati Bengals

Cleveland Browns

Pittsburgh Steelers

THE BROWNS ADVANCED TO THE PLAYOFFS IN 2020. IT WAS THE TEAM'S FIRST POSTSEASON APPEARANCE SINCE 2002.

BECOMING THE BROWNS

The Browns began play from 1946 to 1949 as part of the All-America Football Conference. They won the league championship during all four of those seasons. Then the Browns joined the NFL and played in the NFL Championship Game during their first six seasons in the league. They won three of the championship games. The team is named after Paul Brown, the team's co-founder and original coach. They are the only team in the NFL with no logo or number on their helmets.

IN NINE SEASONS WITH THE BROWNS, FULLBACK MIKE PRUITT SCORED 52 TOUCHDOWNS.

BY THE NUMBERS

FOUR
NFL Championships for the Browns (in the pre–**Super Bowl** era)

423
points scored by the team in 1946—a Browns record!

12
wins for the Browns in 1986—the most since becoming part of the NFL!

17
Browns enshrined in the Pro Football Hall of Fame

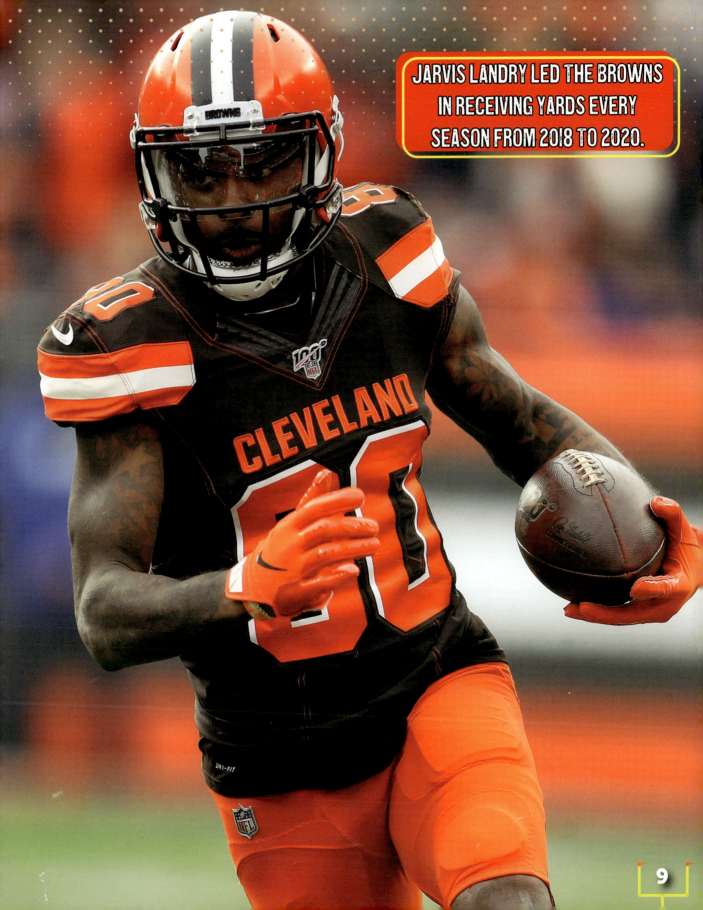

JARVIS LANDRY LED THE BROWNS IN RECEIVING YARDS EVERY SEASON FROM 2018 TO 2020.

FANS IN CLEVELAND PULL FOR THE TEAM EVERY YEAR IN HOPES OF SEEING THE BROWNS ADVANCE TO THE SUPER BOWL FOR THE FIRST TIME.

The Browns play their home games in Cleveland, Ohio. Before 1999, they played in Municipal **Stadium**, which they shared with the Cleveland Indians Major League Baseball team. Since then, the Browns have played at FirstEnergy Stadium. The building usually holds about 67,000 people. But 73,718 piled into FirstEnergy Stadium for a 2002 game against the Pittsburgh Steelers. Hungry fans can enjoy a gourmet burger or bratwurst from the B Spot restaurant inside the stadium.

We're Famous!

In the 2014 movie *Draft Day*, Kevin Costner plays Sonny Weaver Jr., the general manager of the Cleveland Browns. The movie takes place on the day of the NFL Draft. Sonny must decide which trades and draft picks to make. He's hoping to satisfy Browns fans and the (fictional) team owner.

UNIFORM

BROWN

WHITE

Truly Weird

After the 1995 season, the owner of the Browns moved the team to Baltimore. Their name was changed to the Ravens. For three seasons, the team ceased to exist. But in 1999, the Browns were reborn as an **expansion team** and football returned to Cleveland. Some of the players from the 1995 Browns were still on the Ravens rosters when the Browns started play again in 1999!

Alternate Jersey

Sometimes teams wear an alternate jersey that is different from their home and away jerseys. It might be a bright color or have a unique theme. The Browns wore jerseys with orange numbers for an October 2020 game against the Dallas Cowboys. Wearing the alternate jerseys, the Browns came out on top at 49–38.

THE SEATING AREA BEHIND THE EAST END ZONE OF THE BROWNS STADIUM IS CALLED THE "DAWG POUND," AND FANS TAKE THE NAME VERY SERIOUSLY.

Going to a game at FirstEnergy Stadium can be a blast. The stadium's east end is reserved for the "Dawg Pound," one of the most well-known cheering sections in all of sports. Fans often dress in dog-related outfits and sometimes cheer by barking! The Browns also have one of the largest fan groups, called Browns Backers Worldwide. The group has fans in 15 different countries. While the team doesn't have a cheerleading squad, Chomps, the team's costumed mascot, roots on the Browns at every game. Chomps is a Labrador retriever who loves his team! The Browns also have a live mascot, a 125-pound Bullmastiff named SJ.

CHOMPS

HEROES OF HISTORY

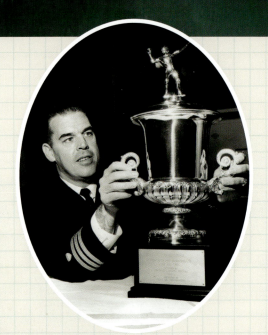

Otto Graham
Quarterback | 1946–1955

During Graham's ten seasons, the Browns played in the NFL Championship Game every year, winning seven times! He led the league in passing yards five times. A **Hall-of-Famer**, Graham was chosen by the NFL as one of the 100 greatest players of all time.

Lou Groza
Offensive Tackle/Kicker | 1946–1959, 1961–1967

Groza was chosen for nine **Pro Bowls** as an offensive tackle. "The Toe" was also the most powerful and skilled kicker in the sport. After retiring in 1959, he came back as a kicker for seven more seasons. The award for each season's best collegiate kicker is named after Groza.

Ozzie Newsome
Tight End | 1978–1990

Known as "The Wizard of Oz," Newsome was one of the greatest receiving tight ends of all time. The all-time leading receiver in team history, he reeled in 662 catches for 7,980 yards in his career. He was elected to the Hall of Fame in 1999.

Joe Thomas
Offensive Tackle | 2007–2017

The Browns selected Thomas with the third overall pick in the 2007 NFL Draft, and he went on to start every one of his 167 career games. Thomas is the only offensive lineman to be chosen for ten consecutive Pro Bowls. He retired in 2017.

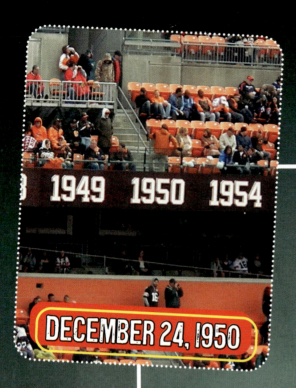

DECEMBER 24, 1950

In their first season in the league, the Browns win the NFL Championship, defeating the Los Angeles Rams, 30–28.

Behind 489 passing yards from Bernie Kosar, the Browns defeat the Jets 23–20 to advance to the AFC Championship Game.

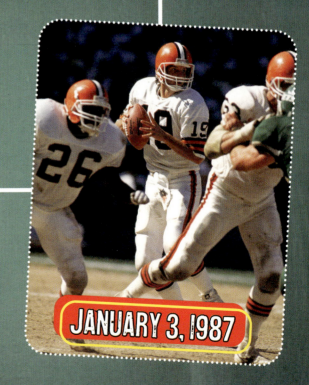

JANUARY 3, 1987

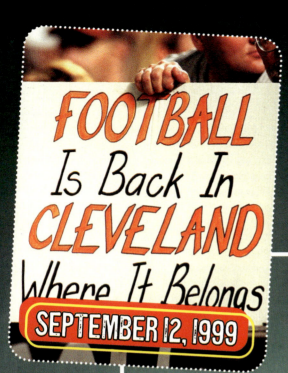

SEPTEMBER 12, 1999

After a three-year absence from football, the Browns return to the NFL. They lose to the Pittsburgh Steelers 43–0.

The Browns defeat the Pittsburgh Steelers 24–22 to earn their first trip to the **playoffs** since 2002.

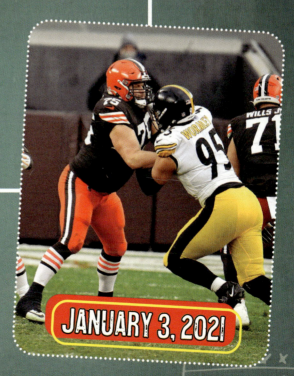

JANUARY 3, 2021

MODERN-DAY MARVELS

Nick Chubb
Running Back | Debut: 2018

Chubb has led the Browns' rushing attack each year since being picked in the second round of the NFL Draft. He gained more than 5,500 total yards during his first four seasons and earned three trips to the Pro Bowl.

Amari Cooper
Wide Receiver | Debut: 2022

The Browns traded for Cooper before the 2022 season in hopes of adding a big-play threat to their passing game. He's pictured here in his Cowboys uniform. Cooper gained more than 1,000 yards receiving in five of his first six seasons in the NFL. He has been chosen for the Pro Bowl four times.

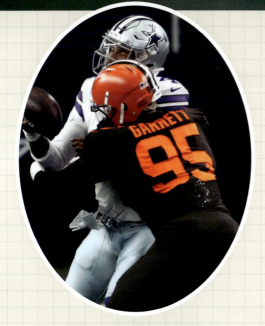

Myles Garrett
Defensive End | Debut: 2017

Since being selected first overall in the NFL Draft, Garrett has been a menace to opposing quarterbacks. Through his first five seasons, Garrett had 58.5 **sacks** and 11 forced fumbles. He earned three trips to the Pro Bowl during that time.

Baker Mayfield
Quarterback | Debut: 2018

Mayfield won the Heisman Trophy as college football's best player in 2017. Then Mayfield threw 27 **touchdown** passes as a **rookie** in 2018. That's the second most all-time for a first-year player. In 2020, Mayfield led the Browns back to the playoffs for the first time in 18 seasons.

IN HIS NINE SEASONS WITH THE TEAM, JIM BROWN SCORED A COMBINED 126 TOUCHDOWNS.

JIM BROWN

Brown is considered by some the greatest running back in NFL history. He led the league in rushing in eight of his nine seasons, and he finished his career with 12,312 yards rushing. His 106 rushing touchdowns are the sixth-most all-time. Brown was named to the Pro Bowl every season of his career and won the **Most Valuable Player** Award three times. He was elected to the Pro Football Hall of Fame in 1971.

FAN FAVORITE

Bernie Kosar–Quarterback
1985–1993

Kosar is beloved by Browns fans who remember that he led the team to the playoffs in his first five seasons with the team. Kosar also led the Browns all the way to the AFC Championship Game three times.

#1

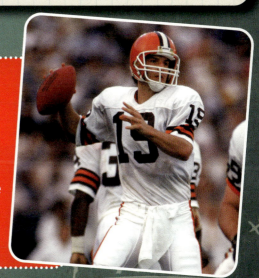

THE BIG GAME

DECEMBER 27, 1964 – NFL CHAMPIONSHIP GAME

Coming into 1964, the Browns had missed out on the postseason for five straight seasons. But after a 10–3–1 finish, the Browns earned a spot in the NFL Championship Game against Johnny Unitas and the Baltimore Colts. No one scored in the game's first two quarters. But Browns quarterback Frank Ryan connected with Gary Collins for three touchdowns in the second half. Jim Brown ran for 114 yards, and Browns defenders intercepted Unitas twice. The Browns won the NFL Championship 27–0.

THE BROWNS' 27-0 WIN OVER THE COLTS WAS ONE OF ONLY SIX SHUTOUTS IN THE HISTORY OF THE NFL CHAMPIONSHIP GAME.

PAUL BROWN LED THE BROWNS TO 158 VICTORIES AND SEVEN LEAGUE TITLES.

AMAZING FEATS

6 Touchdowns in a Single Game

In 1951 by
RUNNING BACK
Dub Jones

10 Interceptions

In 2001 by
CORNERBACK
Anthony Henry

16 Receiving Touchdowns

In 2007 by
WIDE RECEIVER
Braylon Edwards

30 Field Goals

In 2008 by
KICKER
Phil Dawson

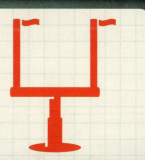

ALL-TIME BEST

PASSING YARDS

Brian Sipe
23,713

Otto Graham
23,584

Bernie Kosar
21,904

RUSHING YARDS

Jim Brown
12,312

Leroy Kelly
7,274

Mike Pruitt
6,540

RECEIVING YARDS

Ozzie Newsome
7,980

Dante Lavelli
6,488

Mac Speedie
5,602

SACKS*

Bill Glass
77.5

Clay Matthews
75

Jerry Sherk
70.5

SCORING

Lou Groza
1,608

Phil Dawson
1,271

Don Cockroft
1,080

INTERCEPTIONS

Thom Darden
45

Warren Lahr
44

Clarence Scott
39

*unofficial before 1982

QUARTERBACK BRIAN SIPE
LED THE BROWNS TO 57
VICTORIES FROM 1974 TO 1983.

GLOSSARY

division (dih-VIZSH-un): a group of teams within the NFL who play each other more frequently and compete for the best record

expansion team (ek-SPAN-shun TEEM): a new team added to the league

Hall of Fame (HAHL of FAYM): a museum in Canton, Ohio, that honors the best players in NFL history

league (LEEG): an organization of sports teams that compete against each other

Most Valuable Player (MOHST VAHL-yuh-bul PLAY-uhr): a yearly award given to the top player in the NFL

playoffs (PLAY-ahfs): a series of games after the regular season that decides which two teams play in the Super Bowl

Pro Bowl (PRO BOWL): the NFL's All-Star game where the best players in the league compete

rookie (RUH-kee): a player playing in his first season

sack (SAK): when a quarterback is tackled behind the line of scrimmage before he can throw the ball

stadium (STAY-dee-uhm): a building with a field and seats for fans where teams play

Super Bowl (SOO-puhr BOWL): the championship game of the NFL, played between the winners of the AFC and the NFC

touchdown (TUTCH-down): a play in which the ball is brought into the other team's end zone, resulting in six points

FIND OUT MORE

IN THE LIBRARY

Bulgar, Beth and Mark Bechtel. *My First Book of Football.*
New York, NY: Time Inc. Books, 2015.

Jacobs, Greg. *The Everything Kids' Football Book, 7th Edition*.
Avon, MA: Adams Media, 2021.

Sports Illustrated Kids. *The Greatest Football Teams of All Time*.
New York, NY: Time Inc. Books, 2018.

Wyner, Zach. *Cleveland Browns*. New York, NY: AV2, 2020.

ON THE WEB

Visit our website for links about the Cleveland Browns:
childsworld.com/links

Note to parents, teachers, and librarians: We routinely verify our web
links to make sure they are safe and active sites. Encourage your
readers to check them out!

INDEX

ABOUT THE AUTHOR

Josh Anderson has published over 50 books for children and young adults. His two boys are the greatest joys in his life. Hobbies include coaching his sons in youth basketball, no-holds-barred games of Apples to Apples, and taking long family walks. His favorite NFL team is a secret he'll never share!